Can the **EVIL SICKLIES** be defeated?

'My class absolutely **LOVED** it!'
REBECCA AND YEAR THREE AT
ST BARNABAS SCHOOL

Prepare for the
SLIMIEST ADVENTURE ever!

'The **FUNNIEST** bunch of **GOO** in the

OXFORD
UNIVERSITY PRESS

Great Clarendon Street, Oxford OX2 6DP
Oxford University Press is a department of the University of Oxford.
It furthers the University's objective of excellence in research, scholarship,
and education by publishing worldwide. Oxford is a registered trade mark
of Oxford University Press in the UK and in certain other countries

Database right Oxford University Press (maker)

First published 2018

British Library Cataloguing in Publication Data

Data available

ISBN: 978-0-19-276377-8

1 3 5 7 9 10 8 6 4 2

Printed in China

Paper used in the production of this book is a natural,
recyclable product made from wood grown in sustainable forests.
The manufacturing process conforms to the environmental
regulations of the country of origin.

WELCOME TO THE
WORLD OF
SLIME

SIX AWESOME LEVELS TO EXPLORE

Enter a team into the great **GUNGE GAMES**. There are loads of slimy sports to take part in, and win!

Leap from platform to platform, to reach the dizzying heights of the **CRUSTY CRATER**. Whatever you do, don't look down.

It's a dash to the finish line as you speed around this ultimate racing circuit. Can you reach **SLIME CENTRAL** in one piece?

Battle it out in a mission to capture the **FUNGUS FORT**. Beware: you'll need more than ninja skills to defeat the enemies on this level.

Can you escape from the **MONSTROUS MAZE**? Just when you think you're on the right track, the ghostly Gools will be ready to attack.

Dare you enter the dungeon of slime? Watch your step or you just might end up stuck in the **BOG OF BEASTS**!

THE STORY SO FAR

After accidentally **sneezing** all over his tablet computer, Max found himself whisked inside his favourite app, **WORLD OF SLIME**, where he came face-to-face with the Goozillas, a group of green, **slimy** creatures he had created in the game.

When Max discovered that his **sneeze** had destroyed the **GOLDEN GLOB**—a magical artefact that keeps the **WORLD OF SLIME** goo flowing—and that without it the Goozillas' volcano home would completely dry out, he teamed up with his icky new friends and set off to retrieve all the missing pieces, hoping to fix the **GOLDEN GLOB** and bring back the **slime**.

Unfortunately, a group of **cutesy-wootsy**, **sickly-sweet** animals from the neighbouring **World of Pets** app—fed up of having to **dress up** and play on **rainbows** all the time—decided they were going to move in to the **slime** volcano.

If the evil Bubble Kitten and her band of Sicklies get the **GOLDEN GLOB** pieces, then it's the end for the Goozillas, and so thanks to that one fateful **sneeze**, Max has found himself in a frantic race not just to save his new friends, but all of **WORLD OF SLIME** itself!

MEET THE GOOZILLAS

JOE
The joker of the gang. Equipped with special slime-seeking gadget glasses.

GLOOP
The first Goozilla that Max created, and his favourite by far.

ATISHOO
A teeny, baby Goozilla, with an enormous sneeze.

GUNK
A mean, green, fighting machine!

BIG BLOB
Supersized, and super strong, but definitely not super smart.

CAPTAIN CRUST
Old, crusty, and in command.

and the sicklies

BUBBLE KITTEN

The evil leader of the Sicklies. She can blow bubble kisses to trap her enemies.

SUGAR PAWS PUPPY

Bubble Kitten's faithful sidekick. His sticky paw prints will stop you in your tracks.

GLITTER CHICK

Watch out for her eggs-plosive glitterbomb eggs.

DREAMY BUNNY

Beware of her powerful hypnotic gaze.

SQUEAKY GUINEA PIG

His supersonic screech will leave your ears ringing.

SCAMPY HAMSTER

The ultimate kickass, street-fighting, rodent.

CHAPTER ONE

SNEEZE, PLEASE

Max ducked, narrowly avoiding a wet sponge that had been flying towards his face. Amy, his little sister, stuck her tongue out at him from the other side of the car's bonnet, then she screamed as Max sprayed her with the hose.

'Aaargh! Dad! Max is **SKOOSHING** me!'

'Max, stop soaking your sister,' said Dad. He was at the back of the car, leaning over to scrub the roof. It was Saturday afternoon, and they'd been washing the car for at least an hour, yet somehow it didn't seem to be any cleaner than it was when they started.

'She threw a sponge at me first!' Max protested.

Dad rolled his eyes. 'Amy, don't throw sponges at your brother.'

'Not fair!' muttered Amy, stamping her foot and crossing her arms.

Max sprayed her again. He couldn't resist.

'Aaaaaargh!' she screamed, and Max laughed as she turned and ran back into the house.

'Sorry!' he said. 'Total accident, honest!'

Dad shot Max a stern look over the top of the car, then sighed in a good-natured sort of way. 'Oh well, looks like it's just you and me, Max,' he said. 'Still, it'll be nice to get some quality father and son time,' he added, before his eyes went wide. 'Wait! What time is it?'

'About four o'clock,' Max replied. 'Why?'

'The Grand Prix is on!' Dad yelped, tossing his sponge back into the bucket. 'Do me a favour and finish off, will you, Max? I'll be back in an hour or so.'

And with that, he ran into the

house, leaving a shocked, stunned, and ever-so-slightly damp Max holding the hose.

'Uh, yeah. OK. I suppose,' said Max, but the door had already slammed closed. Max continued spraying the car, muttering under his breath. 'So much for "quality father and son time",' he said.

The water **SpLAsHED** against the windows, making little rainbows above the car as Max moved around it. When he reached the back, he spotted something on the back seat.

'The tablet!' said Max. He remembered Amy using it when they were out in the car earlier.

Max glanced at the front door of the house. Dad wasn't going to be back for an hour or so, and Amy was so wet Mum would probably put her in the bath—although Max had never understood how a bath was supposed to help when you were already soaked. That meant that Max wouldn't be disturbed for a while.

He shut off the hose, dropped it onto the driveway, then clambered into the back of the car. The windows were still covered in foamy water, making it impossible for anyone to see inside the car from the house.

Picking up the tablet, Max pushed the power button. The home screen appeared, with all the apps neatly lined up. The slimy face of a Goozilla smiled out from the **WORLD OF SLIME** icon in the centre of the screen. Amy's World of Pets app was right beside it.

On the World of Pets icon, looking all wide-eyed and adorable, was the game's main character—Bubble Kitten. Of course, Max knew the kitten was secretly the leader of 'the Sicklies'—a wicked bunch of pets who wanted to take over the Goozillas world for themselves—and nowhere near as cute as she looked.

Tapping the **WORLD OF SLIME** icon, Max waited for the image of the slime volcano to load, then wrinkled his nose, trying to conjure up a **sneeze**. One good blast of **nose-goo** on the screen was all it took to magically transport him into the app. Unfortunately, he'd recovered from his recent cold, and no matter how much he poked and prodded at his nostrils, no **sneezes** came.

Last time, he'd used a feather to tickle his nostrils until he'd **sneezed**, but there were no feathers around. What there was, though, was the brown paper bag their fast food lunch had come in. Max rummaged around inside, and found a handful of little paper sachets. Most of them were salt, but in amongst them was what he'd been hoping to find.

'Pepper!' said Max. He tore open the pepper sachet, took a pinch of it, and **SPRINKLED** it into his nostrils. Immediately, his nose began to **WRIGGLE** and **TWITCH**.

'AAAH . . .
AAAH . . .

AAAT

A thin spray of snot went **SPLUT** on the screen. Around him, the car felt as if it were spinning and spiralling. His chair seemed to ripple, becoming softer and stickier.

And then, the whole world flipped inside-out and upside-down, and Max found himself *HURTLING* through darkness.

CHAPTER TWO

SOFT LANDING

Max **THWUMPED**, face first, into a wall. Luckily, it was quite a soft wall, and he **BOINGED** off it, then landed on the floor, unharmed.

'Wow,' he said, sitting up. 'Pity I don't have airbags for crash landings like those.'

Max looked at the wall he'd bumped into, and realized it wasn't actually a wall, at all. A perfect imprint of his face could be seen in the gooey green surface of the Goozilla, Big Blob. Max had hit roughly where Big Blob's bum would have been, if the Goozillas had bums.

'MAX IS BACK!'

cheered a voice from behind him. Max
recognized it as belonging to Gloop, the first
Goozilla he'd ever created.

12

He turned to find Gloop and the other Goozillas *RUSHING* towards him. Or most of them were *RUSHING*, at least. Captain Crust, the oldest of them all, was hobbling along on his **SNOTSHOOTER** cane. His dry, crusty body meant he moved much more slowly than the others, but he saluted from the back as the other green blobs rushed to surround Max.

'And just in time, too,' said Joe, his eyes sparkling excitedly behind his Gadget Glasses. 'We found another piece of the **GOLDEN GLOB**!'

Max gasped. The **GOLDEN GLOB** was the power source for the Goozillas' slime volcano. It was what kept the slime flowing and stopped the whole place drying up.

Max's first **sneeze** had broken it and **SCATTERED** it across the volcano's many levels, and now he was determined to help his friends get it back.

'You did? Before Bubble Kitten?' asked Max.

Gunk snorted and gripped his **SLUDGESPUTTER 6000** gun tightly. 'Sure did. I guess that kitty ain't so smart after all.'

'**AMAZING!**' cheered Max. This was great news. Bubble Kitten had always been one step ahead in the past, but now the shoe was on the other foot. Max looked around. 'So, where's the **GLOB** piece?'

'It's in there,' said Gloop, pointing to a metal sphere about the size of a basketball that sat on the floor nearby.

'You sure?' said Max. 'It doesn't look big enough.'

'It's funny you should say that,' said Joe. 'Look around. Does this place look familiar?'

Max looked around him. He thought he knew every level in the slime volcano, but he didn't recognize this place at all. It was just a big, mostly empty cave, with the sphere, some junk, and something a bit like a photo booth standing a few metres away.

15

Around the metal ball was . . . actually, Max wasn't quite sure what it was. It looked like a model someone had made out of junk. Bits of pipe, planks of wood, and other random rubbish had been linked together forming a winding, weaving sort of spiral shape.

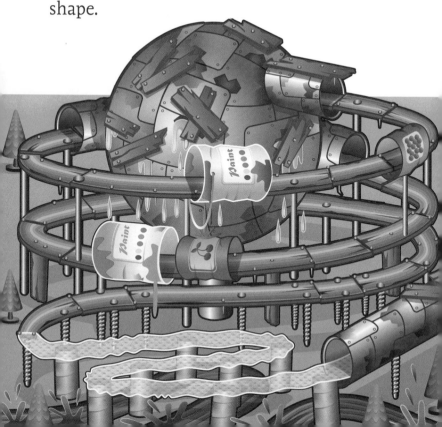

It had all been painted in bright colours and was sitting on a square of fake grass, with some little plastic trees dotted around it. The sphere was in the centre of the model. A length of rusty metal pipe was inserted into it through a hole, and while there was something familiar about the set-up, Max couldn't quite place it.

'Nope,' he admitted. 'No idea.'

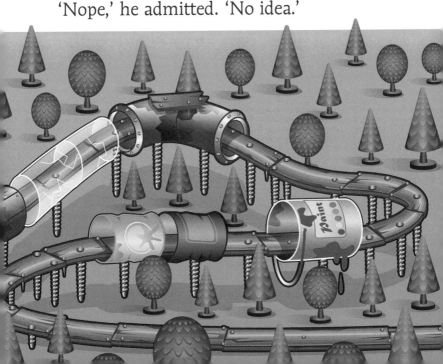

'It's **SLIME CENTRAL**,' wheezed Captain Crust, hobbling up to join the others. Atishoo, the smallest Goozilla, perched on the captain's hat. He smiled happily and gave Max a welcoming wink.

Max frowned. 'You mean like in the **RACE** *to* **SLIME CENTRAL** level?' he said. 'But that's a driving game. It's got tracks and obstacles and cars and stuff. This is just a load of old junk and a photo booth. It's nothing like it.'

Joe and Gloop both caught one of Max's arms each and half carried, half dragged him towards the booth. 'Not yet,' said Joe, as they bundled Max inside. 'But just wait.'

Joe and Gloop squeezed in behind him,

followed by Gunk and Captain Crust, with Atishoo still on his hat.

'See that button?' said Gloop. His face was squished against Joe, making his voice muffled. 'Press it.'

'What does it do?' Max asked, studying the little red button on the wall.

'Oh, nothing much,' said Joe, then he giggled. 'Just a little thing, really.'

'Yeah, an absolutely tiny thing!' chirped Gloop.

'Can we hurry this up?' asked Gunk.

Max pressed the button. A strange yellow light illuminated the inside of the box, and Max felt his insides turn to jelly.

He was about to ask what was going on when something zapped him in the chest and the inside of the booth

SUDDENLY BEGAN TO GROW!

CHAPTER THREE

A TINY THING

It took Max a few seconds to realize that he was wrong. The booth wasn't growing, he was shrinking!

'WHAAAAA!'

he yelled as he and the Goozillas were zapped down to ant-size. The booth, which had been a tight squeeze a moment ago, now stretched out for miles in every direction. The lino floor had become a vast desert of black and white checks.

Max was about to ask the Goozillas what was going on when a wind suddenly whipped up around them all. Specks of dust the size of rocks flew past him, and Max had to throw his hands in front of his face to protect himself.

'**OH, NOW WHAT?**' he cried, and then he was pulled off his feet by the roaring gale. He flipped helplessly, tumbling end over end, before he was sucked into a plastic pipe.

Max flew along the tube for several seconds,

THUMPING and BUMPING off the sides.

'THIS IS GOING TO HURT!' he yelped.

And then, with a **POP** he shot from the end, flailed in the air for a few moments, and hit the ground. To his surprise, he landed on soft grass. Or something very like it.

'Hey, cool! That wasn't so bad after all,' Max said, a split-second before a pile of Goozillas landed on the back of his head, squishing his face into the soil.

'Whoops, sorry!' said Gloop, as the Goozillas rolled off Max's back. Just like Max, they had all been shrunk down and now they all clambered upright, dusting themselves down.

'**THAT WAS AWESOME!**' Joe cheered.
But his excitement turned to a look of
horror as he glanced back towards the pipe
they'd emerged from.

'**LOOK OUT!**' came an echoey cry. But
before the Goozillas had time to run, Big
Blob came rocketing out of the tube, bum
first, scattering them all like skittles.

'Thanks, Big Blob,' Gunk groaned. 'Maybe try warning us a little earlier next time.'

Once Max and the others had pulled themselves upright again, they looked around. A big grin spread across Max's face. 'OK, now I recognize it!' he said. And he did. The grassy area they were standing on was right beside a rainbow-striped road that Max now realized was a plank of brightly-painted wood.

Up close, the fake grass and plastic trees looked almost like the real thing.

'I never knew it was tiny!' Max said. 'But it makes perfect sense. Driving through pipes, dodging tennis balls . . . I thought they were **HUGE**, but they're just normal size. It's the cars that are tiny!'

Joe put a squelchy arm around Max's shoulder and turned him around. 'Speaking of driving,' he said. **'CHECK IT OUT!'**

SPEED

ACCELERATION

WEIGHT

HANDLING

GRIP

Max gave a **YELP** of excitement. The Bogey Bus was parked over near the starting line, only it wasn't the Bogey Bus any longer. It had been given an upgrade, and now had sleek fins, a large spoiler at the back, and flames painted along the side.

'What do you think?' asked Gloop.

'How did you get it shrunk down?' Max asked. 'There's no way that fit inside the booth.'

'Piece by piece,' Gunk said. 'We gave it an upgrade when we put it back together.'

'So I see!' Max cheered. 'It looks

SO FAST!'

'I hope you're right, young Max,' said Captain Crust. 'The fourth **GOLDEN GLOB** piece is located at the end of the course, deep in the heart of **SLIME CENTRAL** itself. The whole **WORLD OF SLIME** depends on us crossing the finish line and claiming the trophy.'

'That shouldn't be too hard,' said Max. He gestured around them. 'It doesn't look like we've got anyone to race against.'

'OH,'

purred an all-too-familiar voice from somewhere nearby.

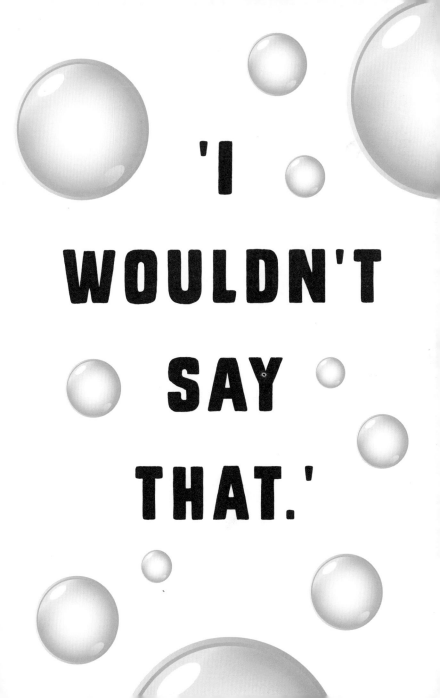

'I WOULDN'T WOULDN'T SAY THAT.'

CHAPTER FOUR

AND THEY'RE OFF!

Bubble Kitten shot out of the shrinking
pipe and managed to flip expertly in the air,
before landing perfectly on all four feet right
beside them.

'Ha! And she nails the landing!' the
kitten boasted, right before a flailing blue
shape slammed into her like a cannonball,
and they both went tumbling across the
grass.

'Whoops! Sorry, boss,' said Sugar Paws,
when they finally rolled to a stop. Bubble
Kitten glared up at the dog, her face covered
in blades of plastic grass. 'Here, let me get

that,' Sugar Paws said, slobbering over her face with his big tongue.

'Get off! Cut it out!' the cat hissed, shoving him away. She got up, shot her sidekick a dirty look, then tried to smile convincingly.

'GOOLOSERS,' said Bubble Kitten.

'WHAT AN UNPLEASANT SURPRISE.'

'Bubble Kitten!' Max growled. 'What are you doing here? Or is that a stupid question?'

'Any question you ask is always a stupid question,' Bubble Kitten sneered.

Sugar Paws Puppy frowned. 'I don't get it.'

Bubble Kitten sighed. 'I'm saying he's stupid.'

'Oh,' said Sugar Paws. 'That's not very nice.'

'Well, of course it isn't nice,' said Bubble Kitten. She turned to the floppy-eared blue dog. 'You do know we're the baddies, yes?'

Sugar Paws's eyes widened. 'Are we? Since when?'

'Since always,' said Bubble Kitten.

Sugar Paws pulled a sort of 'Well, I never'

face, then fell silent.

'But yes, in answer to your stupid question, we're here for the same reason as you,' said Bubble Kitten. 'We want that **GLOB** piece. And we're going to win the race and get it!'

Gunk raised his **_SPLUTSHOOTER_**. 'Or we could goo you right now and stop you going anywhere.'

Bubble Kitten leaned forwards, making her face an inviting target. 'Go right ahead,' she urged. 'If you're too afraid to race me, that is.'

'**AFRAID?**' Gunk snorted. '**OF YOU? NO CHANCE!**'

Bubble Kitten shrugged. 'Oh goody. Then

put down your silly slime gun, and let's settle this on the race track.'

Max could hear an engine purring somewhere nearby. He looked around, trying to work out where it was coming from. 'Uh, can anyone hear something?'

'Ah, yes,' said Bubble Kitten. 'It appears my teammates have arrived. You didn't honestly think you got here first, did you?'

The air was suddenly filled with the revving of powerful engines. A procession of the strangest-looking vehicles Max had ever seen drove out from behind the enormous booth, steered by some all-too-familiar drivers.

'The Sicklies,' groaned Atishoo. 'We should have known.'

The first car was shaped like an egg,

with two large wheels at the back, and two much smaller wheels at the narrower front. Driving it was a wide-eyed yellow bird with sparkles in her feathers.

'You know Glitter Chick, of course,' Bubble Kitten announced. 'I'm sure you haven't forgotten your **EGG-SPLOSIVE** encounter!'

SPEED
▄▄ ▄▄ ▄▄ ▄▄ ▄▄

ACCELERATION
▄▄ ▄▄ ▄▄ ▄▄ ▄▄

WEIGHT
▄▄ ▄▄ ▄▄

HANDLING
▄▄ ▄▄ ▄▄ ▄▄

GRIP
▄▄ ▄▄

Behind Glitter Chick's egg car was a large ball made of clear plastic. Sitting in a little driver's booth inside the ball was Scampy, the ninja hamster they'd faced at Fungus Fort. He steered with two control levers, and glared furiously at the Goozillas as he rolled past.

SPEED

ACCELERATION

WEIGHT

HANDLING

GRIP

Bubble Kitten jumped into the driver's seat of the third vehicle. The engine purred as she drove past Max and the Goozillas. The car was a flashy pink convertible with the roof folded down. The front was designed to look like Bubble Kitten's face, with a caged-off area at the back where Sugar Paws now sat.

SPEED

ACCELERATION

WEIGHT

HANDLING

GRIP

It was the fourth car that really caught Max's eye, though. Although he wasn't sure it was a car at all. It was more like a little bowl on wheels, but with four pipes attached to it. The pipes started up near the driver's seat, then curved backwards, becoming large **FOGHORN-LIKE** funnels at the back. They could be part of the engine, Max guessed, but then why would one end of each pipe be sticking out of the dashboard?

The driver caught Max watching and puffed out his furry cheeks. He was a golden brown colour, and looked a bit like Scampy Hamster, only **BIGGER**, and without the ninja headband. He looked mean and menacing, but when he spoke, his voice was a high-pitched squeak.

SPEED
▬▬▬▬▬▬▬▬▬▬

ACCELERATION
▬▬▬▬▬▬▬▬▬▬

WEIGHT
▬▬▬▬▬▬▬▬▬▬

HANDLING
▬▬▬▬▬▬▬▬▬▬

GRIP
▬▬▬▬▬▬▬▬▬▬

'Be afraid, weirdoes. Be very afraid!' he said in a shrill chipmunk-like voice. Max and the Goozillas all immediately began laughing.

'What was that?' Joe giggled.

'That was so squeaky it made my ears fall off!' said Max.

'Shut up!' chirped the newcomer. 'Cut it out! Stop laughing!'

This just made the Goozillas worse. They fell about, giggling hysterically. Even Captain Crust enjoyed a snigger behind his moustache.

'Oh, so you think Squeaky Guinea Pig is funny, do you?' Bubble Kitten sneered from the driver's seat of her car. 'We'll see how much you laugh when we get the **GLOB** piece.'

'Look lively, chaps!' said Captain Crust, ushering the others over to the upgraded Bogey Bus. 'These ruffians are going to start without us.'

'ALL ABOARD!'

cried Gunk.

'HUP-HUP-HUP! DOUBLE-TIME!'

As Max and the Goozillas clambered into the Bogey Bus, they heard the Sicklies rev their engines. 'Hurry!' Max yelped, sliding onto the chair beside Joe. Seat belts slithered across their laps and clicked into place.

'This is new,' said Joe. He had spotted a little button on a pillar in front of them. A sign above it read:

IN CASE OF EMERGENCY, PRESS HERE.

'Gunk must have added it. I wonder what it does?'

Max opened his mouth to ask Gunk about the button, but the roaring of the engine drowned him out. A sign lit up over by the starting line and began counting backwards from three.

'Everyone hold onto something!' Gunk urged. 'This thing has been

SUPERCHARGED!'

A horn blared. Gunk **SLAMMED** down the accelerator and, with a rattle and a shudder, the Bogey Bus lurched forwards ... and then stopped. The engine coughed and died, and Max could only watch in dismay as Bubble Kitten and **the Sicklies** raced off into the distance.

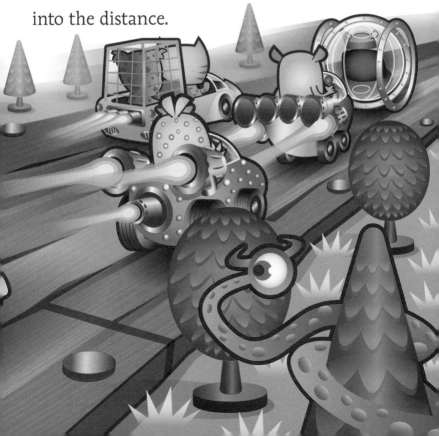

CHAPTER FIVE

FIVE

STUCK!

'What are you doing? Just drive the blasted thing!' cried Captain Crust.

Up front, Gunk fired up the engine and floored the accelerator. The bus lurched forwards again. Smoke poured out from the back wheels. And then, with another **SPLUTTER** and **WHEEZE**, the engine gave up.

Gloop pulled open one of the bus's windows and squeezed his head through the narrow gap. 'Those cheats!' he cried. 'Those dirty cheats!'

'What is it?' asked Atishoo, peering over the brim of Captain Crust's hat. 'What have they done?'

'They've clamped the back wheel,' Gloop said, pulling his head back inside. The top half of him, which had been sticking out through the window, was now much longer and thinner than the bottom half. He shook himself and flobbed back into his normal shape. 'They've trapped us. We can't go anywhere. Not unless we can break through solid metal.'

Everyone thought about this for a moment, then all eyes went to Big Blob. Not only was he the **BIGGEST** Goozilla in history, he was also the **STRONGEST**. He realized everyone was watching him, then his green face went a little red around the cheeks as he blushed.

After reassuring Big Blob that he hadn't farted (or not that they'd noticed, at least), Max explained the problem. The big Goozilla **SQUEEZED** himself out through the bus's door and plodded to the back wheel. He looked down at it for several long, agonizing seconds.

'Well?' barked Gunk. He was all too aware that the Sicklies had a big head start, and were getting further away with every second that passed.

'It's a wheel,' said Big Blob, his voice calling through

the open window.

Gunk rolled his eyes. 'Give me strength.'

'Yeah, we know that, Blob,' Max shouted back.

'It's got a thingy on it.'

'Yes, we know that, too,' Max said. 'Can you take the thingy off?'

There was another pause.

'What thingy?'

Gloop squeezed his top half out through the window again and pointed to the wheel. 'That thingy. The only thingy there! Can you break it off?'

Big Blob took hold of the metal clamp and began pulling. 'It's no use. There's no way I'm going to be able to . . .' he began.

'OH!'

he continued as the clamp snapped as easily as a paper chain. '**I DID IT!**'

'He did it!' cried Max. 'He broke it.'

'Excellent news!' said Captain Crust. 'Now, tell him to get back aboard, quick smart.'

'Oh, what's the point?' Gunk grunted. 'They're too far ahead now. We'll never catch . . .' He looked in his rear view mirror. An **ENORMOUS** green shape was right behind the Bogey Bus. A pair of squelchy hands pressed against the back window. 'What's Blob up to?' Gunk asked, and then he was *SLAMMED* back into his seat as Big Blob gave the Bogey Bus a sudden shove.

The **POWERFUL PUSH**

was just the blast-off they needed. As they **HURTLED** out of the parking area and onto the track, Gunk fired up the engines and gave the accelerator everything he had. The bus's caterpillar treads became a blur as it

ROCKETED

along the rainbow-coloured track, in hot pursuit of the Sicklies.

CHAPTER SIX

THE RACE IS ON!

Max had never been more grateful for a seatbelt in his life. It clung tightly across him as the Bogey Bus streaked up the rainbow ramp, sparks spraying out behind it.

'**GREAT GOOBALLS!**' hollered Captain Crust, holding onto his hat. 'This is too fast!'

'No, it's not fast enough!' said Gunk. He wrenched the wheel left, *SKIDDING* the bus towards an arrow-shaped marking on the road. 'Everyone hold on, I'm going for the boost pad!'

As the bus's front wheels hit the arrow, it lit up in red. Max felt his eyeballs get shoved back in his head as the boost pad *LAUNCHED* the bus onwards, *FASTER* and *FASTER*, until the road was just a blur of solid colour.

'UH,' groaned Gloop.

'I THINK I'M GOING TO THROW UP.'

'**DON'T YOU DARE!**' yelped Atishoo, ducking for cover behind the brim of the captain's hat. 'I'm right behind you!'

Gunk heaved on the wheel again, and everyone screamed as the Bogey Bus screeched around a bend on two tracks. 'I can't look!' cried Joe, covering his eyes.

'Me neither,' agreed Max.

'Nor me!' said Gunk.

All the passengers **GASPED** in fright. Gunk grinned. 'Gotcha. Just kidding!'

The flickering colours of the rainbow road disappeared as the Bogey Bus powered into a long, dark tunnel. Through the windscreen, up ahead, Max could make out a shape trundling along the middle of the pipe.

'**HAMSTER AHOY!**' Gunk announced. 'Dead ahead!'

'Can you get around him?' asked Captain Crust.

'Around? No,' said Gunk, crunching the gearstick and making the bus go even faster. 'Through? Oh yes!'

Up ahead, Scampy Hamster swivelled his seat to face backwards out of his spinning ball. His eyes snapped wide in panic when he saw the Bogey Bus *ROARING* towards him. Frantically, the Sicklie reached for his controls. Max thought he was going to try to get out of the way, but instead something *FLEW* from the back of his spinning ball. Lots of somethings, in fact.

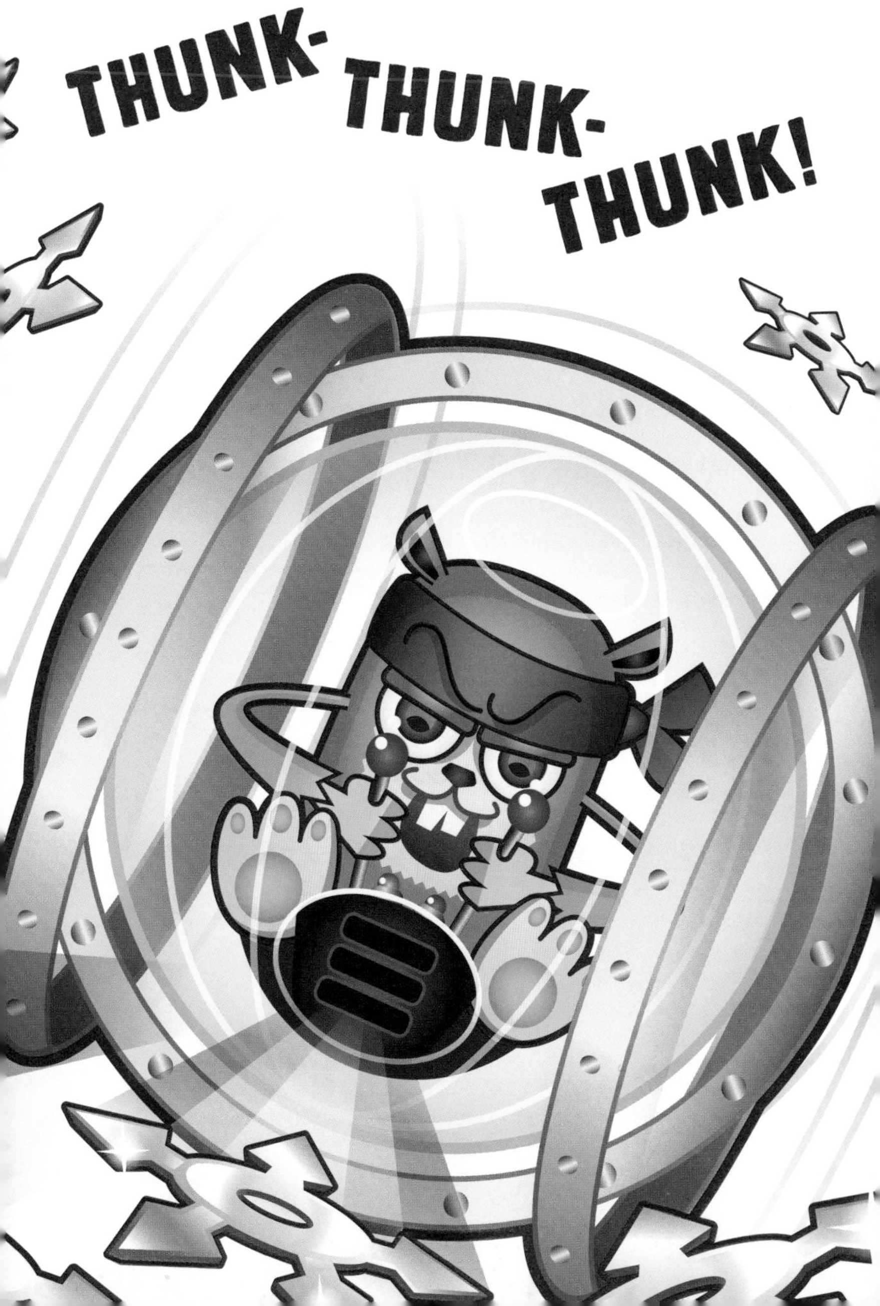
THUNK-THUNK-THUNK!

Three ninja throwing stars hit the windscreen, their pointed blades sticking through the glass.

'**HE'S GOT WEAPONS!**' cried Captain Crust. '**THAT BLIGHTER'S GOT WEAPONS!**'

'We'd better pull back,' Gunk groaned.

Joe activated his Gadget Glasses and peered ahead. 'No. Go right,' he said. 'As fast as you can!'

'**ARE YOU CRAZY? I'M IN A TUNNEL! THERE IS NO RIGHT!**'

'Trust me, Gunk,' Joe said. 'Do it!'

Muttering, Gunk heaved the wheel to the right. The Bogey Bus climbed up the curved wall, just as four more throwing stars **WHIZZED** below it. Gunk **SLAMMED** the accelerator all the way to the floor and continued steering right.

The Bogey Bus was going

TOO FAST

for gravity to catch up. It climbed all the way up the wall until it was driving on the ceiling.

Down below, Scampy Hamster gazed up in disbelief as the Bogey Bus drove past above him, upside down. The Goozillas all waved through the sunroof as the bus

ROARED

over Scampy's head, before it banked back down the tunnel wall.

'**WE DID IT!**' Gloop cheered. 'We overtook him!'

'But he's taking aim with more of those blasted star things!' said Captain Crust, staring out through the back window.

'We'll see about that,' said Gunk. He pressed down on the brake and the bus slowed down. Behind them, Scampy frantically tried to stop, but it was too late. There was a crack as his plastic ball smashed into the back of the bus, and Scampy was launched out of his seat.

Scampy hit the back windscreen with a **THUNK**. There then followed a long, drawn-out **SQUEEEEEAK** as he slid slowly down the glass and landed in a heap on the ground.

There was a roar as Gunk gunned the engine, and the Bogey Bus rejoined the race.

CHAPTER SEVEN

PAPER THIN

The exit of the tunnel was dead ahead. The circle of light showing the world beyond the pipe grew steadily larger as the Bogey Bus **STREAKED** towards it.

Bouncing around in the chair next to Joe, Max was deep in thought. He'd played the racing level lots of times, and while there were different types of race you could do, the layout of the track was always the same.

'Rainbow ramp. Tube tunnel,' he muttered. 'What's next?'

Max let out a sudden yelp. 'Of course! Gunk, slow down!'

'Are you crazy?' Gunk yelled back at him. 'We need to catch them up!'

Max pointed ahead at the mouth of the tunnel. 'If you don't slow down, we're all done for. That's **BOG ROLL BRIDGE**!'

BOG ROLL BRIDGE had caught Max out lots of times in the game. One minute, he'd be racing through the dark tunnel, then he'd be skidding across a flimsy sheet of thin toilet paper, out of control. As soon as he hit the brakes, the tyres would tear through the paper, and he'd plunge into the murky brown river below.

'Oh great, now you tell me!' Gunk groaned. He hit the brakes and the tunnel was filled with a loud **SCREECHING** sound as the Bogey Bus skidded to a stop right at the mouth of the pipe.

BOG ROLL BRIDGE stretched out ahead of them, blowing slightly in the breeze. Max reckoned it had to be the cheapest, nastiest toilet paper in the whole world. It was so thin it was see-through, and Max could make out the outline of the cardboard tubes supporting the bridge like pillars.

'Slow and steady, Gunk,' Atishoo whispered, as Gunk carefully rolled the bus out onto the toilet paper. It sagged beneath them, and everyone held their breath for a few seconds until they were sure it wasn't going to break.

Gloop gulped. 'I never thought I'd say this, but I'm glad Big Blob isn't here.'

The bus crept forwards, rocking back and forth as the toilet paper swung unsteadily. Joe pointed to the button on the pillar in front of him and Max. 'Should I press this now, do you think? This feels like an emergency.'

Max shook his head. 'I don't think so,' he said, gripping his chair. 'Gunk can get us to the other side.'

'Uh-oh,' said Gunk.

Max swallowed. 'What? What's wrong?'

'We've got company,' said Gunk.

Sure enough, up ahead, Max could see an egg-shaped vehicle crawling along even slower than the Bogey Bus.

'Glitter Chick!' said Gloop. The throwing stars in the windscreen were making it difficult to see, so he stuck his head out through the side window again and peered ahead.

A moment later, he brought his head back in. '**GO, GO, GO!**' he cried. '**FLOOR IT!**'

'**WE CAN'T!**' Gunk protested. '**WE MIGHT FALL THROUGH!**'

'She's dropping egg bombs!' said Gloop. 'If we don't get off this bridge, the whole thing is going to come down!'

Gunk stared in disbelief for a few moments, then gritted his teeth.

'RIGHT, THEN. LET'S DO THIS!'

he spat.

Joe grabbed Max. Max grabbed Joe. Captain Crust leaned across and gripped Gloop's arm, while Atishoo held onto the old man's hat. They all held onto each other and **SCREAMED**

as the Bogey Bus *SHOT* forwards, tearing holes in the toilet paper behind its tracks.

AAAAARRRRRRGGGGHHH!!!!!!!

At that speed, the bridge rocked and tilted violently. Gunk wrestled with the wheel, trying to keep them from tumbling right off the paper's edge. Glitter Chick's eggmobile was just ahead of them now. A trail of sparkly eggs was spread out behind the vehicle. A few of them were flashing, suggesting they might explode at any second.

'B'BYE, GOO-LOSERS!'

the little bird bellowed, then the egg-car began to accelerate rapidly, racing for the end of the bridge before it exploded.

'Oh no, you don't!' growled Captain Crust, aiming his **SNOTSHOOTER** cane out through the window. There were a series of **SPUTTING** sounds, then Glitter Chick's car skidded as it hit a patch of slimy **goo**.

The Bogey Bus **ROCKETED** past just as the first egg **EXPLODED**. The toilet tissue broke along a perforated seam and began to swing down behind them. Max felt weightless for a second as the bridge fell away, but then the tracks made it to the wooden plank on the other side, and the bus **ROARED** safely back onto the track.

Behind them, they heard a shout. **'I'LL GET YOU FOR THIS, GOOZILLAS!'**

cried Glitter Chick, followed a moment later by a thick, gloopy splosh.

'WE MADE IT!' Gloop cheered. **'WE ACTUALLY MADE IT!'**

'Nothing can stop us now,' said Gunk.

But he spoke too soon! As the Bogey Bus rounded another bend, they spotted Squeaky Guinea Pig's car dead ahead. Squeaky must have been expecting them, because as soon as the bus came into sight he leaned forwards and placed his mouth over the pipes in his dashboard.

The guinea pig let out a long, ear-splitting **SQUEAK** that sounded like fingernails being dragged down a blackboard. The noise echoed along the pipes, getting louder and louder until it emerged as a concentrated blast of pure sound.

The Bogey Bus's windscreen shattered. Its front end crumpled, and its caterpillar tracks were torn to pieces as the soundwave SLAMMED into the vehicle.

'BRACE FOR IMPACT!' cried Gunk, as the bus began to tip sideways.

'WE'RE GOING TO CRASH!'

CHAPTER EIGHT

IN CASE OF EMERGENCY

Max groaned. Something was . . . strange. It took him a moment to figure out what it was.

He was upside-down. The Goozillas were upside-down, too. And so, now he came to think about it, was the bus.

'Is everyone in one piece?' asked Captain Crust, his voice even more shaky than usual.

'I think so,' said Gloop.

The bus lurched suddenly. There was a loud **CRASH** as it rolled another few metres and came to a stop, right way up, and back on its caterpillar tracks again.

'Hey, we're back in the race!' cried Gunk, right before all four sets of tracks fell off and the bus collapsed onto the ground. 'Nooooo! I spoke too soon.'

Gunk **SLAMMED** his fist on the horn, but it only let out a faint **PARP**. 'Now Bubble Kitten will get the **GLOB** piece. We're done for.'

Max felt Joe's elbow nudging him in the ribs. 'Now?' Joe asked.

At first, Max didn't know what Joe was asking, but then he remembered the In Case of Emergency button. He shrugged. 'Why not? I don't suppose it can do any harm.'

Joe nodded. 'OK, here goes,' he said. He pressed the button.

Nothing happened.

86

'Well, that was disappointing,' Joe muttered, before he and Max were suddenly *ROCKETING* sideways as the window swung outwards and their seat was *LAUNCHED* out through the side of the Bogey Bus.

They clung to each other and **SCREAMED** as the seat changed shape beneath them. Handles unfolded. Wheels clicked into place.

By the time the seat had hit the ground, it was no longer a seat at all. Joe's side had transformed into a sleek motorcycle, while Max's had become a sidecar. A goo-gun was fixed to the front of the sidecar. It swung around to the rear, and back again as Max waggled the joystick.

SPEED

ACCELERATION

WEIGHT

HANDLING

GRIP

'Whichever one of you guys added this, you're a genius!' cried Joe. He and Max both looked back at the broken Bogey Bus. Gunk and the others were pointing ahead along the track.

'Get going!' Gunk urged.

'Get the **GLOB** piece!' added Gloop.

Joe twisted the grip of his handlebars and the bike's engine *REVVED*. 'OK, then,' he said, narrowing his eyes. 'Let's do this!'

The motorcycle pulled a dramatic wheelie as it *SPED* off. Max thought he heard the other Goozillas **WHOOPING** and **CHEERING**, but then the howling of the wind became too loud.

The scenery whipped past them so quickly Max didn't realize where they were on the course until it was almost too late.

'Tennis balls!' he warned, as six enormous balls bounced down the track towards them.

'On it,' replied Joe, leaning low in his seat. The bike dodged and weaved through the tennis ball avalanche, Joe's Gadget Glasses helping him plot a safe route.

They were soon gaining on Squeaky Guinea Pig, who had slowed down to make it past the bouncing balls. When he heard them coming,

Squeaky leaned forwards and puffed out his cheeks as he wrapped his lips around one of the pipes.

This time, Max could actually see the sound wave that emerged. It rushed backwards towards him and Joe, a fast-moving ripple in the air. Joe leaned sideways and

the
sound
wave
SCREAMED
past.

'**LOOK OUT!**' Max yelped as another blast of solid sound **ROCKETED** towards them. Joe twisted the handlebars and leaned left, this time. Max clung to the sidecar as it was lifted off the ground. The sound wave shrieked past just beneath the sidecar's wheels, then Max was thrown around as Joe **SLAMMED** the sidecar back on the ground again.

'Looks like he's going for a big one,' Joe warned. Sure enough, Squeaky had opened

his mouth wide enough to cover all of the pipes this time. The Guinea pig took an **ENORMOUS** breath. He puffed out his cheeks until they were the size of peas. This doesn't sound like much, but considering the size he'd been shrunk to, it was **HUGE**.

'Not this time!' said Max, taking aim with the sidecar's goo-gun. He fired four shots, each one blocking up one of the pipes—and just in time.

Squeaky squealed into the pipes, but the sound had nowhere to go. All four pipes exploded with a **BANG** and the guinea pig's car began skidding and weaving all over the road.

Even over the sound of the engine and the howling wind, Max heard Squeaky's cry of **'OH NO!'** as his car skidded off the road and *SLAMMED* into the grassy embankment beside it. Max and Joe cheered as they *ROCKETED* past the wreckage of the vehicle, and the dazed guinea pig inside it!

And then Max and Joe were suddenly plunging down a steep hill, their wheels a blur beneath them. **'IT'S NOT FAR TO SLIME CENTRAL!'** Max shouted.

'And there's Bubble Kitten,' said Joe,

twisting the bike's grip and forcing the engine to work even harder. The pink convertible car was dead ahead. Max could see Sugar Paws sitting in the back, staring ahead.

'EAT OUR DUST, SICKLIES!'

Joe cried, as the bike **SPED** past. 'We're going to make it, Max! We're going to win the race and get the **GLOB** piece!'

Max joined in the cheering, but then stopped. The car's front seat was empty. Sugar Paws was driving using a steering wheel mounted in the back.

'She's not there!' said Max. 'Bubble Kitten isn't there!'

'What?' spluttered Joe. 'Well, where is she, then?'

A shadow fell across the track, as

if the sun had been blocked out.

Max looked up.

And up.

And up.

There, towering high above them, was Bubble Kitten. Somehow, she had changed back to normal size which meant, to Max and Joe, she was now a **GIANT**.

'OH, GOODY,' the cat purred, in a voice that made the whole track shake.

'I DO SO LOVE A GOOD CHASE!'

CHAPTER NINE

BIG CAT ON THE LOOSE

'*F-FASTER*, Joe, *FASTER!*' Max
stammered.

'I'm going as fast as I can!' Joe told him.
The bike was making a scary **SCREAMING**
noise, its engine rattling like it might
explode at any second. It was no use,
though—Bubble Kitten was gaining quickly,
her **ENORMOUS** paws booming like
thunder on the ground behind them.

'She must have deliberately left the race!'
said Joe. 'So that, if we managed to get past
everyone else, she could stop us! She knew
she couldn't beat us fair and square.'

'But she won't fit into **SLIME CENTRAL**,' Max pointed out.

'She doesn't have to,' said Joe. 'She just needs to make sure *we* don't, then Sugar Paws can get the **GLOB** piece.'

'HERE I COME, READY OR NOT!'

Bubble Kitten laughed, her pink tongue hungrily licking her lips.

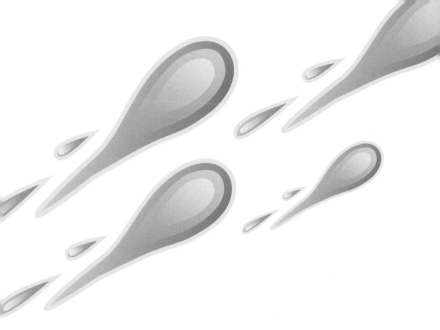

'I don't usually like to eat anything too gooey, but I might make an exception this time.'

A paw swiped at them, claws extended. Max opened fire with the bike's goo-gun, spraying sticky pellets of snot-like slime at the oncoming paw. Bubble Kitten pulled it back, spitting and hissing in disgust, and the bike pulled further ahead.

'Think you're clever, do you?' the cat growled. 'Let's see you dodge this!'

Drawing in a deep breath, she prepared to blow one of her inescapable bubble traps. Moving quickly, Max took aim with the gun again. He squeezed the trigger and held it down, sending a powerful spray of gunge straight into the cat's half-open mouth.

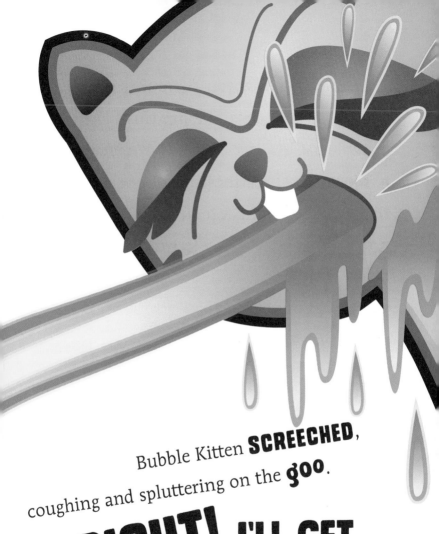

Bubble Kitten **SCREECHED**,
coughing and spluttering on the **goo**.

'RIGHT! I'LL GET YOU FOR THAT!'

She **POUNCED** after them, her paws tearing up the track. The mouth of the tunnel that led into *SLIME CENTRAL* was just a few hundred metres in front of them, but the cat was gaining too quickly. There was no way they were going to make it!

With an excited cry, Bubble Kitten

LUNGED

for the bike.

Her front paws had almost caught them when she suddenly **JERKED** to a **STOP** in mid-air. She wailed in pain, and the hair on her back stood on end as she began to fall towards the ground.

The cat's vast shadow grew **LARGER** around the motorbike. 'Hurry! Faster!' Max yelped. The bike shot forwards just as Bubble Kitten crashed down, shaking the ground like an

EARTHQUAKE.

'What happened?' asked Joe.

Leaning around in his seat, Max caught a glimpse of Big Blob standing behind the fallen kitty, holding onto her tail.

'SEE?'

Blob called after them.

'I TOLD YOU I'D CATCH UP!'

'Big Blob happened!'

Max barely had time to give their rescuer a wave before the bike raced into the tunnel and up the final slope. Max could see the dome-like ceiling of *SLIME CENTRAL* up ahead, and there was the **GOLDEN GLOB** piece, floating in the air right in the centre.

That was the good news. The bad news was that besides a narrow ledge running around the outside, the whole bottom half of the metal sphere was filled with bubbling slime.

'We won't be able to reach it,' Max said. 'It's too high!'

Joe took one hand off the handlebars and tapped his Gadget Glasses. Lots of little angles and mathematical symbols flashed up behind the lenses, then a grin spread across his slimy face.

'Oh, I think we will,' Joe said, and he reached into the sidecar and grabbed Max just as the bike hit a speed boost ramp. They both **SCREAMED** as they were launched forwards at *EYE-WATERING SPEED*, and

FIRED into the air.

Max, Joe, and the bike all **TUMBLED** above the **BUBBLING** pit of **goo**. The bike, being heavier, began to fall first. There was a gloopy

SPLOT *as it tumbled into the* **slime,**

as Joe and Max hurtled upwards and onwards. The **GOLDEN GLOB** piece was dead ahead now.

There was another **SOGGY** sound as the shimmering shard passed through Joe's body and got stuck somewhere inside.

For a moment, Joe seemed to glow a brilliant shade of gold and then, with a thunk, he and Max hit the wall on the other side of *SLIME CENTRAL*, and slid down onto the ledge.

They lay there for quite a long time, getting their breath back. As their breath returned, they first began to snigger, and then began to giggle. Soon, the sound of their laughter echoed around the huge metal sphere.

'YOU DID IT!'

a voice cried, echoing inside the dome.

'Way to go, guys!' chimed another.

Joe and Max both sat up to see the other Goozillas running out of the tunnel. Big Blob scooped up Captain Crust and they all hurried around the ledge to join Max and Joe.

'Uh, thank you, Big Blob,' said the captain. 'You can put me down now. There's a good chap.'

Captain Crust was placed carefully in front of Max. 'Good show, chaps!' he said. 'Looks like we did it again.'

Joe patted his tummy and the golden glow of the **GLOB** piece shone inside him. 'Yep!' he said. 'Looks like we did!'

Before they could celebrate any further,

Max heard the sound he'd really come to hate over the past few days.

BEEP-BEEP-BEEP!

It was his screen time alarm. His time inside the **WORLD OF SLIME** was over for another day.

'Uh-oh, looks like I have to go,' Max said.

He grinned at Joe. 'Great driving!'

'I couldn't have done it without you,' Joe replied.

A terrible thought occurred to Max. 'Wait! I'm tiny. Will I still be this size when I go back home?'

Gloop shrugged, and gave a nervous smile. 'Well, I guess there's only one way to find out!'

Max **GASPED** and sat forwards suddenly, as if waking from a dream.

It took him a moment to figure out where he was. He was sitting in the back of the family car, the tablet resting on his knees.

115

Suddenly, the door was **YANKED** open beside him, making him yelp with fright. Amy was there, the hose held in her hand and a furious expression across her face.

'Give me the tablet, or I'll soak you!' she said.

'Don't! You'll soak the whole car!' Max warned. 'Here, take it!'

He thrust the tablet into his sister's hand and she lowered the hose. For a moment, her face lit up with excitement, but then she frowned.

'HEY! WHAT HAPPENED TO BUBBLE KITTEN?'

Amy cried.

Max got out of the car and looked at
the screen. Bubble Kitten was still on the
World of Pets icon, but her tail was now
wrapped in bandages, and there was a large
sticking plaster on her chin where it had
SLAMMED into the track.

'I don't know,' said Max, fighting the urge
to giggle. 'But I bet it's driving her crazy!'

JOIN MAX AND THE GOOZILLAS ON THEIR OTHER ADVENTURES IN THE
WORLD OF SLIME

OUT NOW

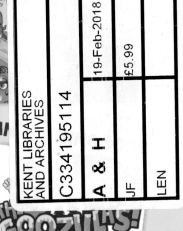